CLEVELAND RADIO PLAYERS

Original adaption and Performances

Originally adapted for the radio and performed by The Cleveland Radio Players. Directed by Milton Matthew Horowitz. Recorded at Bad Racket Studios.

Original adaption and Performances

Originally adapted for the radio and performed by
The Cleveland Radio Players. Directed by Milton
Matthew Horowitz. Recorded at Bad Racket Studios.

                            Starring:

Denny Castiglione   The Voice of the
                               Cleveland Radio Players

        Eric Sever   ADMIRAL RICHARD E BYRD

   Jack Matuszewski   CAPTAIN RICHARD E BYRD

      Dina Kralnik   THE NURSE

    Andrew Jurcak   HOWIE THE RADIO MAN

       Kat Kenny   THE ARIANI HOST

       Jack Hunt   THE NEPHEW

   Jack Matuszewski   THE ARIANI LEADER

Into the North

By

Milton Matthew Horowitz

INTO THE NORTH

CAST

ADMIRAL BYRD
          (narrator)
Admiral Richard Evelyn Byrd is a an
aortic explorer and military navy
Admiral

CAPTAIN BYRD
the same man as the admiral only
back in the 40's when he was just a
Captain.

HOWIE THE RADIO MAN
admiral Byrds co-pilot and radio
operator his name is Howie

BASE CAMP COMM
base camp radio communication

ARIANNI HOST
inner-world host and escort to the
leader

ARIANNI LEADER
leader or speaker for the sentient
inner-earth

DOCTOR
A Doctor at a mental institute that
seems crooked and dishonest

NURSE
A nurse who works under the crooked
doctor mentioned above

NEPHEW
Admiral Richard Byrds Nephew and
publisher of the Admirals secret
Diary

OPENING CREDITS

THE VOICE OF THE CLEVELAND RADIO PLAYERS
Hello this is the voice of the
Cleveland Radio Players my name is
Denny Castiglione Ladies and
Gentlemen

DRUM ROLL INTRO

                    THE VOICE OF THE CLEVELAND RADIO PLAYERS
and your listening to the Cleveland
Radio Players Performance of
"title" based on the secret diary
of Admiral Richard E. Byrd Written
and directed By Milton Matthew
Horowitz.

MENTAL INSTITUTE

                    ROLL IN NURSING HOME MUSIC
                                   HI HEEL SHOES APPROACH

                    NURSE
                (condescending)
Hello Admiral... how are we feeling
today? ... did ya get good rest?

                    ADMIRAL BYRD
as an Admiral in the Navy we slept
only when needed.

                    NURSE
well then Admiral you should enjoy
the long hours we reserve for you
to sleep...

                    ADMIRAL BYRD
I'm an explorer and a military man
this is no place for retirement
this is an above ground cemetery

                    NURSE
now Admiral watch that mouth or Ill
have to recommend you for seclusion
and we both know how you hate that

                                   FOOT STEPS APPROACHING

                    DOCTOR
nurse I need you to get this room
tidy right away the Admiral has a
visitor coming any minute

                    NURSE
Yes Doctor I'll get right on
that...

                    DOCTOR
see that you do and when you're
finished here... come to my office
I have some uh tidying that needs
to be done in there as well

                    NURSE
Yes Doctor I'll be right there

                                        FOOTSTEPS AWAY

                    NURSE
now Admiral isn't that nice you
have a visitor coming

                    ADMIRAL BYRD
Probably some Military mongrel sent
here to shut me up... you know they
wont be able to hide the truth
forever

                    NURSE
Listen Admiral the reason your here
is because the government doesn't
trust you to be alone especially
with all the crazy stuff you been
saying...

                    ADMIRAL BYRD
It's not crazy it's one hundred
percent true... every word of it...
some day you'll see

                    NURSE
I'm sorry Admiral but I don't think
anyone is going to believe you
about a superior race of beings
that live in the middle of the
earth mmmmkay...

                    ADMIRAL BYRD
not while I'm locked up here they
wont... why do you think they sent
me here?! ... it's an attempt to
discredit me should I say anything
contrary to their narrative...

                    NURSE
that's enough Admiral, your gonna
get yourself all worked up and were
gonna have to tranquilize you
again, you don't want that now do
ya

                    ADMIRAL BYRD
I dare you to try you little minks
I'll break your... ffffff--

                    NEPHEW
Uncle Ricard? it's me Harry...
whats all the commotion about in
here

                    ADMIRAL BYRD
Shes trying to kill me

                    NURSE
your Uncle has a very creative
imagination I should say

                    NEPHEW
Well that's Uncle Richard for
you... have you been telling naval
stories again?

                    ADMIRAL BYRD
there not stories its all true...

                    NURSE
     (condescending)
of course they are Admiral... I'll
leave you two alone I'll be back
later for his medication

                              FEMALE FOOTSTEPS AWAY

                    NEPHEW
seems like they've been taking
great care of you around here Uncle
Richard

                    ADMIRAL BYRD
They are just waiting for me die
Harry... Listen to me there's
something I want you to do for me
that's very important...

                    NEPHEW
sure... anything Uncle Richard

                    ADMIRAL BYRD
look here... I stash it under my
mattress... I have my original
flight log from my first flight
over the north pole

                    NEPHEW
sure I know the one you read it to
me as a kid...

                    ADMIRAL BYRD
Not that flight log that was the
official report I had to turn in,
this is the REAL flight log I took
that day

                    NEPHEW
what?... but... that means you lied
on an official government document?

                    ADMIRAL BYRD
sure to a civilian it's lying but
to the government its all part of
the plot... you don't understand
they made me...

                    NEPHEW
who? the navy or the military?

                    ADMIRAL BYRD
the Navy the Military all of 'em

                    NEPHEW
Under what administration?

                    ADMIRAL BYRD
Administration? pick one?

                    NEPHEW
what are you saying?

                    ADMIRAL BYRD
Coolidge, Hoover, Roosevelt,
Truman, they're all the same take
your pick it doesn't make any
difference what matters is that I
have the original flight log here
now

                    NEPHEW
well I can't do anything with that
now? what if I get court marshaled
conspiring?... and your in an
institute ya know... they're just
gonna say your crazy

                    ADMIRAL BYRD
don't you think I know that... why
do you think they put me here...

                    ADMIRAL BYRD
listen to me... I'm going to finish
the story by re-writing it here in
my secret diary and when I pass I'm
going to leave it for you right
here under this mattress... make
sure you get your hands on it first
and publish it for me once it's
safe...

                    NEPHEW
Uncle Richard I don't know if I
can--

                    ADMIRAL BYRD
Promise me... promise me you'll
publish this book for all to see...
I have too many secrets in me and I
don't want this one to die with
me... once you read it... I know
you'll agree with me...

                    NEPHEW
OK... OK I promise Uncle Richard
I'll take it to a publisher...

                    ADMIRAL BYRD
Be sure that you do, please come
back soon... I know it wont be long
now...

                    NEPHEW
please don't talk like that--

               FEMALE FOOTSTEPS

                                        DOOR CREAK/OPEN

                    NURSE
Hello Admiral I'm back with your
medication... it's medication time
Admiral

                    NEPHEW
look I'm gonna get going but I'll
be back soon to check on you...

                    ADMIRAL BYRD
Thank you Harry... and as for you
Nurse I'd like a light left on and
some stationary I want to take some
notes on some bible passages I was
reading

                    NURSE
very well admiral

                    NEPHEW
see ya Uncle Richard

                    ADMIRAL BYRD
bye Harry remember what we talked
about

                                        FOOTSTEPS AWAY

                    NURSE
here you go admiral a little
something to help you sleep...

                    ADMIRAL BYRD
is that you got? sleeping pills...
it's gonna take a lot more then
that to get rid of me...

                    NURSE
Just shut up and take the pill old
man or I'll call the orderly's

                                        FOOTSTEPS APPROACHING

                    DOCTOR
Nurse I thought I told you make
medication time earlier today...

                    NURSE
I did Doctor the Admiral here is
the last one and he seems to be
disagreeable about taking his
medication

                    DOCTOR
did you threaten him with orderly's

                    NURSE
I did doctor he was just about to
take his medication elementarily I
believe

                    ADMIRAL BYRD
fine I'll take the dam pill... hand
me that glass of water

                    SLIDING GLASS ON TABLE
                    DRINKING SFX

                                        GLASS ON TABLE

                    ADMIRAL BYRD
there happy...

                    NURSE
Good night Admiral, see you in the
morning...

              FOOTSTEPS AWAY X 2
                 DOOR CLOSE
               FOOTSTEPS FADE
                  SPIT SFX

                                    PILL FALL SFX

                    ADMIRAL BYRD
I'm not takin' any dam sleepin'
pills... alright now where was I?

                              PAPER SFX SCRIBLING SFX

                    ADMIRAL BYRD
oh yeah that's right... the
introduction...

                              INTRO MEMOIRS MUSIC

                    ADMIRAL BYRD
                 (V.O.)
I must write this diary in secrecy
and obscurity. It concerns my
Arctic flight of the nineteenth day
of February in the year of Nineteen
and Forty Seven. There comes a time
when the rationality of men must
fade into insignificance and one
must accept the inevitability of
the Truth! I am not at liberty to
disclose the following
documentation at this writing...
perhaps it shall never see the
light of public scrutiny, but I
must do my duty and record here for
all to read one day. In a world of
greed and exploitation of certain
of mankind can no longer suppress
that which is truth.

                                    MUSIC FADES

FLIGHT LOG - BASE CAMP ARCTIC - 2/19/1947

AIRPLANE ENGINE SFX

                    ADMIRAL BYRD
               (V.O. both young and old
               voice)
          Oh-six-hundred hours- All
          preparations are complete for our
          flight north ward and we are
          airborne with full fuel tanks at
          oh-six-ten Hours.

                    SCRIBING SFX

                              ROUGH IDLE SOUND

                    ADMIRAL BYRD
               (V.O.)
          oh-six-twenty Hours- fuel mixture
          on starboard engine seems too rich,
          adjustment made and the Pratt
          Whittneys are running smoothly.

                         ENGINE IDLE SMOOTH

                    CAPTAIN BYRD
          we've been flying for about ten
          minutes now Howie... pretty smooth
          flight conditions... when is our
          next radio check?

                    HOWIE
          approximately an hour and ten
          minutes...

                    CAPTAIN BYRD
          ok good... until then we'll just
          keep our course, I have us trimmed
          for straight and level flight but
          lets keep an eye on the instruments
          anyway

                    HOWIE
          Rodger that...

                              FADE OUT

INT. AIRCRAFT

FADE IN ENGINE IDLE

          ADMIRAL BYRD
what time are we lookin' at Howie?

          HOWIE
it's almost oh-seven-thirty hours
time to make the radio check...

          RADIO SQUELCH
radio check, radio check, come in
base camp this is co-pilot Howie
with Captain Richard Byrd calling
in for our radio check... were
maintaining a heading of thirty six
at twenty three hundred feet...
straight and level flight all
instrumentation seems normal

          BASE CAMP COM
Rodger that radio check your
reception is normal maintain your
heading and report any changes

          HOWIE
Rodger that base camp, maintain
heading and report any
changes...over

          END RADIO SQUELCH

                              SCRIBBLING SFX

          ADMIRAL BYRD (V.O.)
Oh-seven-thirty hours- Radio Check
with base camp. All is well and
radio reception is normal.

          HOWIE
uh... Captain...

          CAPTAIN BYRD
what is it Howie

          HOWIE
I think I see a trickle of oil on
the starboard cowling

          CAPTAIN BYRD
what?!... Where!?... Oh I see...
what does the oil pressure
indicator say?

                    HOWIE
Normal readings

                    CAPTAIN BYRD
you're right...

                    HOWIE
what are we gonna do

                    CAPTAIN BYRD
well I tell you what were not gonna
do and that's turn around... we've
come this far already... lets just
keep an eye on it if it starts to
make us feel uneasy will turn
around and call for help...

                    ADMIRAL BYRD
          (V.O.)
Oh-seven-forty hours- Note...
slight oil leak in starboard
engine, oil pres sure indicator
seems normal, however.

                         ENGINE SHUTTER/TURBULENCE

                    HOWIE
It's getting a little rough up here

                    CAPTAIN BYRD
you're right I don't wanna stress
the airframe too much I'm going to
descend till I find smoother air

               DESCENDING AIRCRAFT

                                   ENGINE IDLE

                    CAPTAIN BYRD
Ah there we go... much better

                              SCRIBBLING SFX

                    ADMIRAL BYRD
          (V.O.)
Oh-Eight-hundred Hours- Slight
turbulence noted from easterly
direction at altitude of 2321 feet,
correction to 1700 feet, no further
turbulence, but tail wind
increases, slight adjustment in
throttle controls, aircraft
performing very well now.

                    CAPTAIN BYRD
Howie I think its almost time for
our next radio check why don't you
call it in while I take a sextant
reading...

                    HOWIE
Aye Captain... Come in base camp
this co-pilot Howie ceiling for a
radio check we've descended to 1700
feet to smoother air still headed
on bearing thirty six

                    ADMIRAL BYRD (V.O.)
Oh-Eight-fifteen Hours- Radio Check
with base camp, situation normal.

                    TURBULENCE DESCENDING AIRCRAFT

                    CAPTAIN BYRD
Turbulence again... I'll climb back
up maybe the winds aloft have
calmed down...

                    ENGINE IDLE SMOOTH SCRIBBLING SFX

                    ADMIRAL BYRD
                 (V.O.)
Oh-Eight-Thirty Hours- Turbulence
encountered again, increase
altitude to 2900 feet, smooth
flight conditions again.

                    HOWIE
we've been flying for about three
hours now captain and all I can
still see is ice and snow below...

                    CAPTAIN BYRD
I agree Howie this particular
flight as been pretty
dismal...Wait! I see something...
just there look... Its like a
Yellow stripes in the snow below...
they seem to be congruent and
linear in nature...

                    HOWIE
What do you think is captain?

                    CAPTAIN BYRD
I don't know but look more colors
in the snow its like a reddish

CAPTAIN BYRD
purple ring in the snow I'm gonna
fly around a fixed point here...
hold this bank while I take some
notes... call in the radio check...

RADIO SQUELCH

HOWIE
Base camp this is co-pilot Howie
calling in for our radio check
we've altered our course to inspect
some coloration in the ice and snow
bleow great lines of yellowish snow
encircled in reddish purple rings
blow... executing two full circles
and returning to assigned heading

BASE CAMP COM
Rodger that radio check two full
circles and return to assigned
heading

SCRIBBLING SFX

ADMIRAL BYRD
          (V.O.)
Oh-nine-ten Hours- Vast Ice and
snow below, note coloration of
yellowish nature, and disperse in a
linear pattern. Altering course for
a better examination of this color
pattern below, note reddish or
purple color also. Circle this area
two full turns and return to
assigned compass heading. Position
check made again to base camp, and
relay information concerning
coloration in the Ice and snow
below.

MECHANICAL FAILURES

HOWIE
uh captain... the gauges

CAPTAIN BYRD
my God whats happening?

HOWIE
we've lost all instrumentation...

                 CAPTAIN BYRD
take a bearing with the sun compass

SCRIBBLING SFX

                 ADMIRAL BYRD
         (V.O.)
Oh-nine-ten Hours- Both Magnetic
and Gyro compasses beginning to
gyrate and wobble, we are unable to
hold our heading by
instrumentation. Take bearing with
Sun compass, yet all seems well.
The controls are seemingly slow to
respond and have sluggish quality,
but there is no indication of
Icing!

                 HOWIE
Captain look up ahead... I looks
like the peak of a mountain...

                 CAPTAIN BYRD
A new mountain range... amazing...
lets not get our hopes up lets wait
to confirm until we get closer

SCRIBBLING SFX

                 ADMIRAL BYRD
         (V.O.)
Oh-nine-fifteen Hours- In the
distance is what appears to be
mountains.

                 CAPTAIN BYRD
maintain this altitude and
heading... I can't believe it... It
doesn't make sense... how could
there be an undiscovered mountain
range...we getting closer Howie
there's no denying it now you see
it too right?

                 HOWIE
of course captain

                 CAPTAIN BYRD
take the controls while I write

SCRIBLING SFX

                    ADMIRAL BYRD
                       (V.O.)
Oh-nine-hundred-forty-nine Hours-
29 minutes elapsed flight time from
the first sighting of the
mountains, it is no illusion. They
are mountains and consisting of a
small range that I have never seen
before!

                                        TURBULENCE

                    CAPTAIN BYRD
I think were on the leeward side of
this mountain range I'm gonna climb
higher

                                   AIRCRAFT ASCENDING

                    ADMIRAL BYRD
                       (V.O.)
Oh-nine-fifty-five Hours- Altitude
change to 2950 feet, encountering
strong turbulence again.

                    CAPTAIN BYRD
can you believe it Howie were about
to fly over the summit of a new
mountain range never before seen by
man

                    HOWIE
OH MY GOD... Captain... look!

                                     EPIC SIGHT MUSIC

                    CAPTAIN BYRD
my goodness... grab the controls

                                    SCRIBLING SFX

                    ADMIRAL BYRD
                       (V.O.)
One Thousand Hours- We are crossing
over the small mountain range and
still proceeding northward as best
as can be ascertained. Beyond the
mountain range is what appears to
be a valley with a small river or
stream running through the center
portion. There should be no green
valley below! Something is
definitely wrong and abnormal here!

                    ADMIRAL BYRD
We should be over Ice and Snow! To
the port-side are great forests
growing on the mountain slopes.

                                        FAILING INSTRUMENTS
Our navigation Instruments are
still spinning, the gyroscope is
oscillating back and forth!

                    HOWIE
Have you ever seen such a beautiful
valley captain... also the
sunlight?... where is it coming
from... I can't seem to spot the
sun...

                    CAPTAIN BYRD
I'm taking us down for a look at
this valley...

               AIRCRAFT DESCEND AND TURN SCRIBING SFX

                    ADMIRAL BYRD
                 (V.O.)
One-Thousand-five Hours- I alter
altitude to 1400 feet and execute a
sharp left turn to better examine
the valley below. It is green with
either moss or a type of tight knit
grass. The Light here seems
different. I cannot see the Sun
anymore.

                                             ENGINE TURN

                    HOWIE
Oh my God Captain is that an
Elephant?

                                        SCRIBBLING SFX

                    ADMIRAL BYRD
                 (V.O.)
We make another left turn and we
spot what seems to be a large
animal of some kind below us. It
appears to be an elephant!

                    HOWIE
that's not an elephant it's... it's
a Woolly Mammoth... descend closer
Captain

AIRCRAFT DESCEND

          ADMIRAL BYRD
        (V.O.)
NO!-It looks more like a mammoth!
... This is incredible! Yet, there
it is! Decrease altitude to 1000
feet and take binoculars to better
examine the animal.

          HOWIE
Its defiantly a woolly mammoth
captain here take a look with the
binoculars... see... you can see
the tusks...

          ADMIRAL BYRD (V.O.)
It is confirmed - it is definitely
a mammoth-like animal! Report this
to base camp.

                    RADIO SQUELCH

          HOWIE
base camp this is Co-Pilot Howie
for a radio check... you're not
gonna believe this but we got a
woolly mammoth here

          BASE CAMP COM
radio check I'm gonna have to ask
you to refrain from telling any
jokes on this com channel

                    RADIO DISTURBANCE

          HOWIE
come in base camp this is not a
joke I repeat not a joke we have a
real life Woolly mammoth below our
aircraft right now...

          RADIO GIBBERISH

                    RADIO STATIC

          HOWIE
the radios are not working
captain... oh this cant be right,
the external temperature reading is
at seventy four degrees
Fahrenheit?... where are we
Capetian?

                    CAPTAIN BYRD
Lord knows I don't...

                                        SCRIBBLING SFX

                    ADMIRAL BYRD
                    (V.O.)
One-thousand-thirty Hours-
Encountering more rolling green
hills now. The external temperature
indicator reads 74 degrees
Fahrenheit! Continuing on our
heading now. Navigation instruments
seem normal now. I am puzzled over
their actions. Attempt to contact
base camp. Radio is not
functioning!

                    HOWIE
OK... now... I thought I was crazy
when I saw the mountain and the
valley and then followed by a
Woolly Mammoth but is that a city I
see on the horizon?

                    CAPTAIN BYRD
I can't even imagine what city it
would be... I have to admit Howie
this is all quite unreal... take
the controls they seem to be barely
effecting the aircraft

                                        SCRIBBLING SFX

                    ADMIRAL BYRD
                    (V.O.)
Eleven-hundred-thirty Hours-
Countryside below is more level and
normal (if I may use that word).
Ahead we spot what seems to be a
city!!!! This is impossible!
Aircraft seems light and oddly
buoyant. The controls refuse to
respond!!

                    ALIEN AIRCRAFT APPROACHING
My GOD!!! Off our port and star
board wings are a strange type of
aircraft. They are closing rapidly
alongside! They are disc-shaped and
have a radiant quality to them.
They are close enough now to see
the markings on them. It is a type

                         ADMIRAL BYRD
of Swastika!!! This is fantastic.
Where are we! What has happened.

                              TRACTOR BEAM

I tug at the controls again. They
will not respond!!!! We are caught
in an invisible vice grip of some
type!

                    RADIO SQUELCH AND CRACKLING
ADMIRAL BYRD
          (V.O.)
Eleven-hundred-thirty-five Hours-
Our radio crackles and a voice
comes through in English with what
perhaps is a slight Nordic or
Germanic accent! The message is:

                    RADIO SQUELCH

                              CUT ENGINE IDLE

ARIANNI HOST
          (radio speaker V.O.)
'vellcome Captain, to our
domain... We shall land you in
exactly seven minutes... Relax,
Captain, you are in good hands.

                    HOWIE
uh Captian... Who's flying the
plane?

                              SCRIBBLING SFX

                    ADMIRAL BYRD
          (V.O.)
I note the engines of our plane
have stopped running! The aircraft
is under some strange control and
is now turning itself. The controls
are useless.

                    RADIO SQUELCH AND STATIC
ADMIRAL BYRD
          (V.O.)
Eleven-hundred-forty Hours- Another
radio message received.

                    ARIANNI HOST
          (radio V.O.)
Vee begin the landing process
now...

AIRCRAFT SHUDDER

SCRIBLING SFX

                    ADMIRAL BYRD
                         (V.O.)
the plane shudders slightly, and
begins a descent as though caught
in some great unseen elevator! The
downward motion is negligible, and
we touch down with only a slight
jolt!

AIRCRAFT LANDS

SCRIBBLING SFX

                    ADMIRAL BYRD
                         (V.O.)
Eleven-hundred-forty-five Hours- I
am making a hasty last entry in the
flight log. Several men are
approaching on foot toward our
aircraft.

MARCHING

They are tall with blond hair. In
the distance is a large shimmering
city pulsating with rainbow hues of
color. I do not know what is going
to happen now, but I see no signs
of weapons on those approaching.

MARCHING HALT

                    ARIANNI HOST
Please exit the aircraft Admiral we
come in peace...

                    ADMIRAL BYRD
                         (V.O.)
I hear now a voice ordering me by
name to open the cargo door. I
comply...

                    ADMIRAL BYRD
                         (V.O.)
From this point I write all the
following events here from memory.
It defies the imagination and would
seem all but madness if it had not
happened.

                 END SCRIBLING SFX
                    AIRCRAFT DOOR OPEN AND CLOSE

END LOG

INNER CITY OF THE ARIANNI

                    ARIANNI HOST
          follow us, right this way

                                        EPIC SCENERY MUSIC

                    ADMIRAL BYRD
                    (V.O.)
          The radioman and I are taken from
          the aircraft and we are received in
          a most cordial manner. We were then
          boarded on a small platform-like
          conveyance with no wheels!

                                        CONVEYOR SFX

          It moves us toward the glowing city
          with great swiftness. As we
          approach, the city seems to be made
          of a crystal material.

                                        SHIMMERING SFX

                    ADMIRAL BYRD
                    (V.O.)
          Soon we arrive at a large building
          that is a type I have never seen
          before. It appears to be right out
          of the design board of Frank Lloyd
          Wright, or perhaps more correctly,
          out of a Buck Rogers setting!

EXT. ARRIANNI PALACE

                                        SCI-FI SFX

                    ARIANNI HOST
          here you must be thirsty you have
          traveled a long way...

                    HOWIE
          do you think we should drink it
          captain?

                    CAPTAIN BYRD
          something tells me if these people
          wanted to kill us they would have
          done it already

                         HOWIE
Good point

                                        DRINKING SFX

                         HOWIE
oh my god its delicious...

                         ADMIRAL BYRD
                    (V.O.)
We are given some type of warm
beverage which tasted like nothing
I have ever savored before. It is
delicious. After about ten minutes,
two of our wondrous appearing hosts
come to our quarters and announce
that I am to accompany them. I have
no choice but to comply. I leave my
radioman behind and we walk a short
distance and enter into what seems
to be an elevator.

                         HOWIE
OK I guess I'll just wait right
here then... nothing scary about
that

INT. ELEVATOR DOWN

                                   ELEVATOR DESCENDING

                         ADMIRAL BYRD
                    (V.O.)
We descend downward for some
moments, the machine stops, and the
door lifts silently upward!

                         ELEVATOR STOP
                                   WALKING DOWN CORRIDOR
We then proceed down a long hallway
that is lit by a rose-colored light
that seems to be emanating from the
very walls themselves!

                         ARIANNI HOST
Halt...

                         ADMIRAL BYRD
                    (V.O.)
One of the beings motions for us to
stop before a great door. Over the

>   ADMIRAL BYRD
> door is an inscription that I
> cannot read.

                    LARGE DOOR OPENING

INT. PALACE OF THE ARRIANI

                         PALACE MUSIC

>   ADMIRAL BYRD
>   (V.O.)
> The great door slides noiselessly
> open and I am beckoned to enter...
> One of my hosts speaks.

>   ARIANNI HOST
> Have no fear, Admiral, you are to
> have an audience with the Master...

                              FOOTSTEPS

>   ADMIRAL BYRD
>   (V.O.)
> I step inside and my eyes adjust to
> the beautiful coloration that seems
> to be filling the room completely.

                    HEAVENLY SIGHT MUSIC

>   ADMIRAL BYRD
>   (V.O.)
> Then I begin to see my
> surroundings. What greeted my eyes
> is the most beautiful sight of my
> entire existence. It is in fact too
> beautiful and wondrous to describe.
> It is exquisite and delicate. I do
> not think there exists a human term
> that can describe it in any detail
> with justice!... My thoughts are
> interrupted in a cordial manner by
> a warm rich voice of melodious
> quality

>   ARIANNI LEADER
> I bid you welcome to our domain,
> Captain...

>   ADMIRAL BYRD
>   (V.O.)
> I see a man with delicate features
> and with the etching of years upon

ADMIRAL BYRD
his face. He is seated at a long
table. He motions me to sit down in
one of the chairs... After I am
seated, he places his fingertips
together and smiles. He speaks
softly again, and conveys the
following

ARIANNI LEADER
We have let you enter here because
you are of noble character and
well-known on the Surface World,
Admiral.

CAPTAIN BYRD
Surface World!...

ADMIRAL BYRD (V.O.)
I half-gasp under my breath!

ARIANNI LEADER
Yes....

ADMIRAL BYRD (V.O.)
the Master replies with a smile,

ARIANNI LEADER
you are in the domain of the
Arianni... the Inner World of the
Earth.... We shall not long delay
your mission, and you will be
safely escorted back to the surface
and for a distance beyond. But now,
Admiral, I shall tell you why you
have been summoned here... Our
interest rightly begins just after
your race exploded the first atomic
bombs over Hiroshima and Nagasaki,
Japan. It was at that alarming time
we sent our flying machines, the
"Flugelrads", to your surface world
to investigate what your race had
done. That is, of course, past
history now, my dear Admiral, but I
must continue on... You see, we
have never interfered before in
your race's wars, and barbarity,
but now we must, for you have
learned to tamper with a certain
power that is not for man, namely,
that of atomic energy. Our
emissaries have already delivered

ARIANNI LEADER
messages to the powers of your
world, and yet they do not heed.
Now you have been chosen to be
witness here that our world does
exist... You see, our Culture and
Science is many thousands of years
beyond your race, Captain...

CAPTAIN BYRD
But what does this have to do with
me, Sir?

ADMIRAL BYRD (V.O.)
The Master's eyes seemed to
penetrate deeply into my mind, and
after studying me for a few moments
he replied,

ARIANNI LEADER
Your race has now reached the point
of no return, for there are those
among you who would destroy your
very world rather than relinquish
their power as they know it...

ADMIRAL BYRD
    (V.O.)
I nodded, and the Master continued,

ARIANNI MASTER
In 1945 and afterward, we tried to
contact your race, but our efforts
were met with hostility, our
Flugelrads were fired upon....Yes,
even pursued with malice and
animosity by your fighter planes.
So, now, I say to you, my son,
there is a great storm gathering in
your world, a black fury that will
not spend itself for many years.
There will be no answer in your
arms, there will be no safety in

ARIANNI MASTER
your science...It may rage on until
every flower of your culture is
trampled, and all human things are
leveled in vast chaos. Your recent
war was only a prelude of what is
yet to come for your race. We here
see it more clearly with each
hour.. do you say I am mistaken?'

                    CAPTAIN BYRD
No... it happened once before, the
dark ages came and they lasted for
more than five hundred years...

                    ARIANNI LEADER
Yes, my son... the dark ages that
will come now for your race will
cover the Earth like a pall, but I
believe that some of your race will
live through the storm, beyond
that, I cannot say... We see at a
great distance a new world stirring
from the ruins of your race,
seeking its lost and legendary
treasures, and they will be here,
my son, safe in our keeping. When
that time arrives, we shall come
forward again to help revive your
culture and your race... Perhaps,
by then, you will have learned the
futility of war and its strife...
and after that time, certain of
your culture and science will be
returned for your race to begin
anew. You, my son, are to return to
the Surface World with this
message...

                    ADMIRAL BYRD
                    (V.O.)
With these closing words, our
meeting seemed at an end. I stood
for a moment as in a dream... but,
yet, I knew this was reality, and
for some strange reason I bowed
slightly, either out of respect or
humility, I do not know which...
Suddenly, I was again aware that
the two beautiful hosts who had
brought me here were again at my
side.

                    ARIANNI HOST
This way, Captain

                                        WALKING AWAY

                    ADMIRAL BYRD
                    (V.O.)
I turned once more before leaving
and looked back toward the Master.
A gentle smile was etched on his
delicate and ancient face.

                    ARIANNI MASTER
Farewell, my son...

                    ADMIRAL BYRD
          (V.O.)
he spoke, then he gestured with a
lovely, slender hand a motion of
peace and our meeting was truly
ended.

                              FAST MISSION MUSIC
Quickly, we walked back through the
great door of the Master's chamber
and once again entered into the
elevator.

INT. ELEVATOR UP

                    LARGE DOOR OPENING

                              ELEVATOR ASCENDING
The door slid silently downward and
we were at once going upward. One
of my hosts spoke again

                    ARIANNI HOST
We must now make haste, Admiral, as
the Master desires to delay you no
longer on your scheduled timetable
and you must return with his
message to your race....

                    ADMIRAL BYRD
          (V.O.)
I said nothing. All of this was
almost beyond belief, and once
again my thoughts were interrupted
as we stopped.

                              ELEVATOR STOP
I entered the room and was again
with my radioman. He had an anxious
expression on his face. As I
approached, I said,

                              MARCHING STOPS

                    CAPTAIN BYRD
It is all right, Howie... it is all
right....

EXT. ARRIANNI PALACE

CONVEYOR SFX

          ADMIRAL BYRD
            (V.O.)
The two beings motioned us toward
the awaiting conveyance, we
boarded, and soon arrived back at
the aircraft. The engines were
idling and we boarded immediately.

AIRCRAFT IDLE

The whole atmosphere seemed charged
now with a certain air of
urgency...

AIRCRAFT DOOR CLOSE

INT. AIRCRAFT

ALIEN LIFT OFF

          ADMIRAL BYRD
            (V.O.)
After the cargo door was closed the
aircraft was immediately lifted by
that unseen force until we reached
an altitude of 2700 feet. Two of
the aircraft were alongside for
some distance guiding us on our
return way....I must state here,
the airspeed indicator registered
no reading, yet we were moving
along at a very rapid rate.

RADIO SQUELCH

          ADMIRAL BYRD
            (V.O.)
Twelve-hundred-fifteen Hours - A
radio message comes through.

          ARIANNI HOST
            (radio speaker V.O)
We are leaving you now, Captain...
your controls are free.... Auf
Wiedersehen!!!!

          ADMIRAL BYRD
            (V.O.)

                         ADMIRAL BYRD
We watched for a moment as the
flugelrads disappeared into the
pale blue sky.

                                    ALIEN CRAFT LEAVING

The aircraft suddenly felt as
though caught in a sharp downdraft
for a moment.

                                          GUSTS OF WIND

We quickly recovered her control.
We do not speak for some time, each
man has his thoughts...

                                             SLOW FADE

ENTRY IN FLIGHT LOG CONTINUES

                     SLOW FADE IN
                   AIRCRAFT ENGINE

                                        SCRIBBLING SFX

                    ADMIRAL BYRD
                      (V.O.)
Twelve-hundred Hours- We are again
over vast areas of ice and snow,
and approximately twenty seven
minutes from base camp...

                 RADIO SQUELCH HOWIE
Base camp this Co-pilot Howie
caling in for a radio check... we
are approximately 100 miles north
of base camp... returning home...
all conditions normal...

                 ADMIRAL BYRD (V.O.)
We radio them, they respond. We
report all conditions normal...
normal...

                              RADIO STATIC DISTURBANCE
BASE CAMP COM
     (excited)
Rodger that radio check one-hundred
miles north and closing in...
maintain your heading... runway
clear for your arrival... (beat)...
good job men!

                    ADMIRAL BYRD
                (V.O.)
        Base camp expresses relief at our
        re-established contact...

                AIRCRAFT DESCEND
                AIRCRAFT LANDING
            AIRCRAFT TAXI AND SHUT OFF SCRIBBLING SFX

INT. AIRCRAFT AT BASE CAMP

                    ADMIRAL BYRD
                (V.O.)
        Thirteen-hundred Hours- We land
        smoothly at base camp. I have a
        mission.....

                    HOWIE
        what are we going to say Captian?

                    CAPTAIN BYRD
        Leave the talking to me

                                        FADE ALL

END LOG ENTRIES.

MARCH 11, 1947

                FADE IN PATRIOTIC MISSION MUSIC
                                        SCRIBBLING SFX

                    CAPTAIN BYRD
                (V.O.)
        March 11, 1947 I have just attended
        a staff meeting at the Pentagon. I
        have stated fully my discovery and
        the message from the Master...

                            TYPEWRITER AND MESSAGING SFX
        All is duly recorded. The President
        has been advised. I am now detained
        for several hours (six hours,
        thirty- nine minutes, to be exact.)
        I am interviewed intently by Top
        Security Forces and a medical team.
        It was an ordeal!!!!

                            INTERROGATION MUSIC
        I am placed under strict control
        via the national security

                    CAPTAIN BYRD
provisions of this United States of
America. I am ORDERED TO REMAIN
SILENT IN REGARD TO ALL THAT I HAVE
LEARNED, ON THE BEHALF OF
HUMANITY!!! Incredible!... I am
reminded that I am a military man
and I must obey orders.

                                          FADE OUT ALL

FINAL ENTRY

                         FADE IN
                       MEMOIR MUSIC

                                      SCRIBBLING SFX

                    ADMIRAL BYRD
             (V.O. fade to old man voice)
These last few years elapsed since
1947 have not been kind... I now
make my final entry in this
singular diary... In closing, I
must state that I have faithfully
kept this matter secret as directed
all these years... It has been
completely against my values of
moral right... Now, I seem to sense
the long night coming on and this
secret will not die with me, but as
all truth shall, it will triumph
and so it shall... This can be the
only hope for mankind... I have
seen the truth and it has quickened
my spirit and has set me free! I
have done my duty toward the
monstrous military industrial
complex... Now, the long night
begins to approach, but there shall
be no end... Just as the long night
of the Arctic ends, the brilliant
sunshine of Truth shall come
again... and those who are of
darkness shall fall in it's
Light... FOR I HAVE SEEN THAT LAND
BEYOND THE POLE, THAT CENTER OF THE
GREAT UNKNOWN....

Admiral Richard E. Byrd United
States Navy 24 December 1956

                  END SCRIBBLING SFX

                                          FADE OUT ALL

MENTAL INSTITUTE

                    FADE IN NURSING HOME MUSICI
                                HI HEELS APPROACHING

                    NURSE
Good Morning Admiral how are we
feeling this morning... still
sleeping I see... Admiral... wake
up... wake up Admiral....

                                    FOOTSTEPS

                    DOCTOR
Good morning Nurse how is the
Admiral this morning

                    NURSE
well he doesn't seem to want to
wake up

                    DOCTOR
My god that because hes Dead nurse!

                    NURSE
Dead?!...nobody told me about
anybody dying when I took this job

                    DOCTOR
Yes! what do you think happens to
people that are retired here

                    NURSE
well I only started a few weeks now
didn't I?... Well at least now that
the Admiral is dead I can spend my
time at work relaxing

                    DOCTOR
uh nurse I hate to tell you but
after the Admiral is taken to the
morgue they're going to bring in
another patient

                    NURSE
you mean there's gonna be more

                                NURSE STARTS TO CRY

                    DOCTOR
there, there now...

                                    FOOTSTEPS

                    NEPHEW
Hello... How's My Uncle Richard?

                    DOCTOR
I'm sorry son but I have bad
news... Your Uncle has passed
away... we were just lamenting over
it ourselves

                    NURSE
huh oh yeah... I'm really sorry
about your Uncle

                    NEPHEW
thank you... may I have a moment
alone with him... do you mind...

                    DOCTOR
Of course... Nurse come lets leave
the Admiral with his Nephew

                    NURSE
Yes Doctor

            FOOTSTEPS MALE AND FEMALE
                                        DOOR CLOSING

                    NEPHEW
I don't know what to say... I just
saw you a few weeks ago... I'm
sorry I didn't visit more... I
don't know what to say about your
mental health or your credibility
in your final days but I will keep
my promise...

                                    COVERS RUSTLING

I'll take your diary to a publisher
as soon as I feel it's safe to... I
loved hearing your old exploration
stories... it's what inspired me to
join the service... I'll read it to
my kids and make sure they read it
to theirs...

                                    DOOR OPENING

                    DOCTOR
I'm sorry to interrupt but the men
from the morgue are here to take
the Admiral...

                        NEPHEW
          I understand... Good Buy Uncle
          Richard I love you...

                                                FOOTSTEPS

                        DOCTOR
          say whats that red book in your
          hands there...

                        NEPHEW
          It's my Uncles secret diary...

                        DOCTOR
          secret diary you say... are there
          any juicy war secrets in there?

                        NEPHEW
          I don't know I haven't read it yet?

                        DOCTOR
          well let me know when you do I have
          a buddy who dabbles in publishing
          ya know...

                        NEPHEW
          I'll keep that in mind... thanks
          for looking after my Uncle... Now
          if you'll excuse me I have to go
          inform the rest of my family...

                    FOOTSTEPS

                                        FADE OUT ALL

END CREDITS

                                    END CREDITS MUSIC

                THE VOICE OF THE CLEVELAND RADIO PLAYERS
          you have been listening to The
          Cleveland Radio Players performance
          of Into The North Pole... written
          and Directed by Milton Matthew
          Horowitz... starring!

                    ERIC SEVER
JACK MATUSZEWSKI
DINA KARALNIK

          ANDREW JURCAK

                    CAT KENNY

                    JACK HUNT
and my name is Denny Castiglione
Ladies and Gentlemen... Into The
North Pole was recorded Live at Bad
Racket Studio... Copyright 2016.

                                        FADE OUT

THE END